Sirko and the Wolf

To Suzanne and Robert
E.A.K.

To Doris and Eric
R.S.

Library of Congress
Cataloging-in-Publication Data
Kimmel, Eric A.
Sirko and the wolf: a Ukrainian tale /
adapted by Eric A. Kimmel;
illustrated by Robert Sauber.—1st ed.
p.   cm.
Summary: A dog and a wolf help each other in time of
need in this Ukrainian tale explaining why dogs and
wolves are forever friends.
ISBN 0-8234-1257-1 (hardcover: alk. paper)
[1. Folklore—Ukraine.]
I. Sauber, Robert, ill. II. Title.
PZ8. 1.k567Si 1997
96-33913 CIP AC
398.2'0947'71—dc20

Designed by Robert Sauber

Sirko
and the
Wolf

A Ukrainian Tale
Adapted by Eric A. Kimmel
Illustrated by
Robert Sauber

Holiday House / New York

Long, long ago, when people first came to the wide, beautiful steppes of Ukraine, a sturdy sheep dog named Sirko lived with a farmer and his family. For many years Sirko guarded his master's flocks from the wolves and other animals.

But the time came when faithful Sirko grew too old to guard anything. The dog spent his days by the stove. "Why do we keep this useless animal?" the farmer's wife complained to her husband. "All he does is eat and sleep. He is good for nothing."

The farmer agreed that his wife spoke the truth. It was time to get rid of their old dog and get a new one.

"Come, Sirko!" the farmer called.

The dog followed his master far out on the steppe. The farmer stopped. He took out his pistol and aimed it at Sirko. Three times the farmer raised the gun and three times he lowered it.

At last he said, "Sirko, my faithful friend, I cannot bring myself to end your life. However, I can keep you no longer. I give you your freedom. Go where you will." He lowered his pistol and walked away.

Sirko threw back his head and began to howl. A wolf heard his
cries and came trotting by.

"Why do you howl so mournfully, Cousin?" the wolf asked.

The dog replied, "I have reason to howl. My master has cast me out. I devoted my whole life to him. Now he abandons me in my old age."

"Why are you surprised?" the wolf asked. "No creature is as ungrateful as a human being. We wolves have told you dogs that for centuries, but you never listened. Even so, I will help you, because we are cousins. I have a plan. It is sure to work."

"Tell me what to do," said Sirko.

"It's very simple." The wolf began to describe his plan to the dog.

The next morning the farmer and his wife went out to harvest the grain. The farmer's wife laid her baby in the shade of a haystack and walked across the field to join her husband in the reaping. Suddenly the wolf sprang out of the tall grass. He seized the baby in his jaws and ran off. The farmer and his wife chased after the wolf, but they were too far away to catch him.

Just then Sirko appeared. "Sirko, save our child!" cried the farmer. The wolf passed close to Sirko. The dog laid back his ears and charged. The wolf turned to meet the attack, but he was no match for the dog — or so it appeared. Snarling and growling, the wolf dropped the baby and ran off. Sirko gently picked up the baby and carried it back to his master.

"Sirko, you wonderful dog!" the farmer exclaimed as he and his wife threw their arms around the animal's neck. "Forgive us for sending you away. You have a home with us for as long as you live."

That evening the farmer's wife cooked a whole platter of dumplings and placed them on the floor, just for Sirko. "Eat your fill, my faithful dog. There is always more if you want it," the farmer said.

Sirko ate until his stomach hurt. Then he lay down to sleep in front of the stove on a goose-down pillow from his master's bed. Never had he known such happiness. *I owe it all to the wolf,* Sirko thought to himself. *Were it not for him, I would be sleeping out on the open steppe tonight with the sky for my roof and the grass for my pillow. The wolf is my true friend.*

The harvest season ended. Winter's first snowfall covered the steppe. Inside their warm house, the farmer and his wife gave thanks for the good things that filled their barn and granary. Sirko the dog slept beside the stove on his goose-down pillow. His paws twitched as he dreamed of running through summer meadows.

One night a distant cry awakened Sirko. It was the wolf, howling on the empty steppe.

The dog remembered his friend. He thought, *I sleep by a warm fire. The wolf makes his bed on the cold ground. I eat my fill from my master's table. What does the poor wolf find to eat? He helped me in my time of need. I must find a way to repay him.*

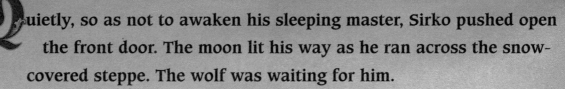

uietly, so as not to awaken his sleeping master, Sirko pushed open the front door. The moon lit his way as he ran across the snow-covered steppe. The wolf was waiting for him.

"Greetings, Cousin! It has been a long time since I saw you," the wolf said. "What brings you out here tonight? Has that ungrateful master cast you out again?"

"Not at all. My master treats me well now, thanks to you," Sirko replied. "That is why I have come. Tomorrow is the harvest festival. My master is preparing a great feast for all his neighbors. I want you to share it with us."

"I am honored," the wolf said. "But what makes you think your master and his friends would welcome me? More likely, they will shoot me on sight."

"No they won't," Sirko said. "I have a plan."

Sirko led the wolf back to his master's house and hid him beneath the table. "Stay here," Sirko told his friend. "When the feast begins, I will beg for tidbits from my master and bring them to you. You can eat as much as you like and stay as long as you please. No one will suspect you are here as long as you keep quiet. Do you understand? You will be perfectly safe, but you must not make any noise."

"Count on me, Cousin. I won't make a sound," the wolf said.

As soon as the sun came up, the farmer and his wife began laying out the food for the harvest feast. There were cakes and pastries, sausages and dumplings, boiled ham and roast pork, chickens, geese, ducks, and turkeys. The wolf's nose twitched with the wonderful smells.

Soon the guests began to arrive. As soon as they were seated, the priest led them in a prayer of thanks. Then the feast began. Sirko trotted back and forth along the table, begging for food.

"Away, dog!" the guests said. "Dogs aren't allowed to beg at the table."

But the farmer told them, "This dog saved our baby from a wolf! He can have anything he wants. The best is none too good for my dog Sirko." The farmer cut the choicest portions from the roast and gave them to Sirko, who brought them to the wolf hiding beneath the table.

"Delicious!" the wolf exclaimed, smacking his lips. The feast went on for hours. Everyone began to feel merry. The wolf felt merry, too.

"Let's have some music," the guests called. The farmer picked up his bandora and began to play. Soon everyone was singing.

"I like this music. I want to sing, too," the wolf told the dog. "I can sing better than these people."

"No!" Sirko pleaded. "Remember your promise. You must not make a sound."

"I want to sing," the wolf insisted.

"Don't!" Sirko begged. "I will bring you more food if you will only be quiet."

"I don't want more food," the wolf said. "I want to sing." With that, he threw back his head and howled. Sirko howled, too, to drown out the wolf's cries.

"Your dog makes a lot of noise," the guests complained to the farmer.

"My dog Sirko can make as much noise as he wants," the farmer said.

The wolf howled louder. Sirko howled louder, too.

"He sounds like a wolf," the priest remarked.

"That's what you think!" the wolf exclaimed. "Listen to what a real wolf sounds like!"

Before Sirko could stop him, the wolf burst out from under the table, howling loud enough to rattle the windows.

The table overturned as the guests scattered in panic. Chairs, dishes, and platters flew everywhere.

"Run for your lives! It's a wolf!" they screamed.

The farmer reached for his musket. "Get back, all of you! Give me a clear shot at him!"

But before he could fire, Sirko charged at the wolf. "Run!" he said. "I will chase you. It is your only chance."

The wolf fled out the door with Sirko at his heels.

By now the other guests had found their muskets. They poured out of the house to shoot at the wolf, too, but the farmer stopped them.

"Don't shoot! You might hit my dog. Put up your guns and come back inside. Leave the wolf to Sirko. My dog Sirko will teach that wolf not to come around here ever again."

Sirko pursued the wolf across the snow-covered steppe. Only when he was miles from the farmhouse, out of sight of the farmer and out of range of the muskets, did he stop.

"I'm sorry I had to chase you. It was the only way to save your life," Sirko told the wolf.

"Think nothing of it, Cousin," the wolf said. "I thank you for that, and for all the good food and the fine company. But I have decided that the homes of human beings are not for me. I don't mind being hungry and cold, as long as I can sing when I please. I would rather be free than fed."

"And my place is with my master," said Sirko. "You and I are different, true, but we are friends just the same. Let us swear a vow that we will be friends forever—as long as people are not around."

So it has been to this day. Whenever dogs hear wolves howling on the steppe, they howl, too. For they still remember that vow. And they still tell this story.

Author's Note

I adapted this story from a version in Irina Zheleznova's collection *Ukrainian Folk Tales* (Kiev: Dnipro Publishers, 1986). My family comes from Kolomyya, a city in western Ukraine, so this story has personal meaning for me, as it does for anyone familiar with the history of that tragic land, so marred by centuries of religious and ethnic strife. The lesson is plain. Like dogs and wolves, people of different backgrounds can live together. They can even become good friends, as long as the masters–kings, czars, and commissars–don't interfere.